World of Reading Pre-1

Disney Junior

Alice's Wonderland Bakery

Wonderful Wonderland Adventures

Adapted by
Catherine Hapka

Based on the episodes
"No Palace Like Home" by **Stuart Friedel**
"Picnic for One" by **Chelsea Beyl**
"Pie Pressure" by **Marisa Evans-Sanden**
"Alice's Stormy Afternoon" by **Marisa Evans-Sanden**
"Try Again Tart" by **Michael Rodriguez**

Designed by
David Roe

DISNEP PRESS

LOS ANGELES • NEW YORK

Contents

No Palace Like Home

Rosa's friends come.
They will stay the night.

Sleeping away from home
is new.

But it is fun!

Rosa comes out.

Tour time!
They look around.

Jabbie comes out.
Jabbie is friendly.

Hattie is scared.

The thrones are different.
The thrones talk.
Hattie is scared.

This is not like home.

But it is fun!

The tour is over.
Rosa takes them to her room.

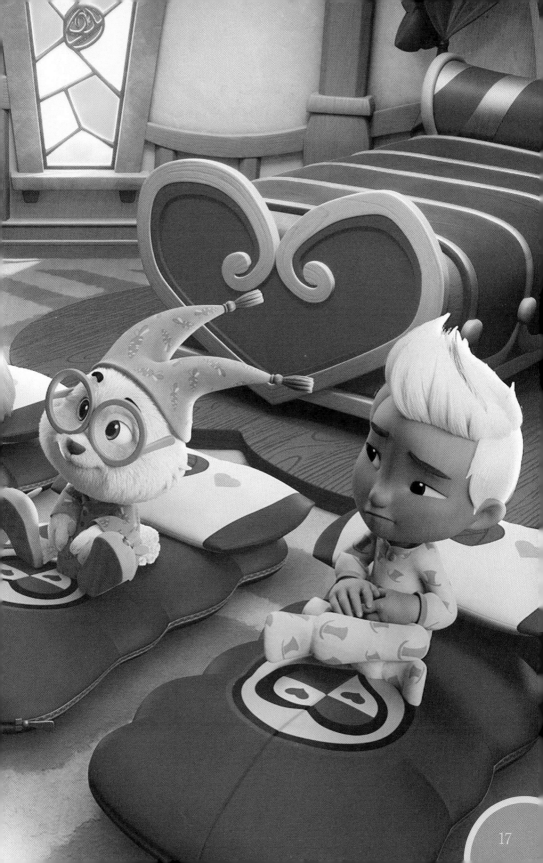

Snack time! Alice eats.

Rosa eats.

Fergie eats.

Hattie does not.

It is different.

They sleep.

Hattie does not.

Jabbie comes in.
Hattie is scared.

Hattie runs.

Alice is up.

Fergie is up.
Hattie is gone.

Time to bake!

Alice bakes.

She bakes a snack.
It smells nice.

Hattie comes back.

Hattie eats.

This is like home!

Picnic
for One

It is picnic day!

Alice bakes.

It looks nice!

Cheshire Cat wants some.

It is for his friends.

Alice bakes.
It looks good!

It is a lot!

He takes the food.

He goes.

The friends go.

They see Cheshire.

He is with his friends.

Who are they?

They look the same.

The picnic starts.

Alice has tea.

Oh, no!

A cup floats!

Time for muffins.

The berries are gone.
Oh, no!

Oh, no!

The hat has eyes!

Time for a bite.

Oh, no!
Where did it go?

What is happening?

Alice knows.

It is Cheshire!

But why?

He wanted friends.

He was sad.

He has friends!
He had friends all along.

Pie
Pressure

The bakery is busy.

Everyone wants pies.

Fergie will help.
Time to bake!

He will bake two pies.

He has to hurry.
Fergie tries.

Dinah will help.

Dinah tries.

It is not easy!

Oh, no!

He has to hurry.

Time to bake.

The pies go in Oven.

Oven has to hurry.

The pies are done.

They are stuck!

They pull.

The pies come apart.

The Queen eats one.

Her face gets stuck!

Cheshire Cat eats one.

He turns red.

Oh, no!

What went wrong?

Fergie knows.

The pies got stuck.

Alice is not mad.
It will be fine.

Time to bake!

They bake a new pie.

The Queen eats it.
She is fine.

Cheshire Cat eats it.

He is fine.

They fixed it!
It is nice to help.

Alice's Stormy Afternoon

Alice is here.
Where are the buds?

The buds are here.
The buds are cute!

The buds are hungry.
Alice will bake.

What will she bake?

The buds
want cupcakes.

Alice is sad.
Cupcakes are too easy.
They are not fun.

Cookie goes out.

Cupcakes are easy.

She knows Alice can do it.

They need ingredients.

They look in the closet.

What is this?
It is fun!

Alice adds it.

The cupcakes are done!

They smell nice.

So nice!

The buds will be glad.

Oh, no! A vine grows.

Oh, no! Another vine grows.

Oh, no! What happened?

Cookie knows.

Alice will fix it.
Time to bake.

But vines are growing!

The vines take her friends.

Alice will fix it.

Alice bakes.
She bakes cakes.

They make it rain.
The vines go away here.

The vines go away there!

The buds are safe!

The cakes taste nice!

Try Again Tart

Alice bakes a treat.

Fergie bakes a treat.

Hattie bakes a treat.

They go to the Queen's home.
They take the treats.

The Queen will taste
the treats.

One treat will win.
They get in line.

They wait for the Queen.

She is here!
Fergie's treat tastes nice.

Alice's treat tastes nice.

Hattie's treat is the best!

He wins!

The Queen wants more.
Hattie has to bake more.

Hattie does not know how.

Alice and Fergie will help.

Alice likes to use steps.

She bakes her way.

Fergie bakes by taste.

He bakes his way.

The treats are not right.

Alice is sad.
This is not fun.

Hattie likes to have fun.
Alice thinks.

She knows what to do.
They will bake Hattie's way!

Alice tells him to bake . . .

but to make it fun!
Hattie bakes his way.

It is just right.

It tastes nice. They did it!